For Selis

Love, Grandpat — J.P.L.

For Leon and Seren with much love

X — A.B.

Text copyright © 2010 by J. Patrick Lewis

Illustrations copyright © 2010 by Ailie Busby

Published in the United States by Schwartz & Wade Books, an imprint of Random House Children's Books,
a division of Random House, Inc., New York.

Schwartz & Wade Books and the colophon are trademarks of Random House, Inc.

Visit us on the Web! www.randomhouse.com/kids

Educators and librarians, for a variety of teaching tools, visit us at www.randomhouse.com/teachers

Library of Congress Cataloging-in-Publication Data
Lewis, J. Patrick.
The kindergarten cat / by J. Patrick Lewis ; illustrated by Ailie Busby. — 1st ed. p. cm.
Summary: A stray cat finds a happy home in a kindergarten classroom.
ISBN 978-0-375-84475-1 (hardcover)
— ISBN 978-0-375-98807-3 (glb)
[1. Stories in rhyme. 2. Cats—Fiction. 3. Kindergarten—Fiction. 4. Schools—Fiction.] I. Busby, Ailie, ill. II. Title. PZ8.3.L5855Kin 2009 [E]—dc22 2008006691

The text of this book is set in Garamond Premier Pro.
The illustrations are rendered in collage, acrylic, pencil, and colored pens.

MANUFACTURED IN CHINA

4 6 8 10 9 7 5 3

First Edition

By J. PATRICK LEWIS

Illustrated by AILIE BUSBY

schwartz & wade books · new york

In a cozy green corner
In a kindergarten room,
A kitty cat napped
By the classroom broom.

With each child sitting
On a carpet square,
Teacher said to the class,
"Take a look over there.

"Mr. Bigbuttons found her
By the jungle gym,

And she wiggled and purred
When he tickled her chin.

"So he brought her inside,
All shivery scared

As if nobody wanted her
And nobody cared.

"She's furry, she's floppy,
Like a raggedy doll,
And her paws are all fluffy,
Like cotton balls.

"Shall we call her Tinker Toy,
Our Kindergarten Cat?
I think she'll be happy
With a name like that."

"Sit, here, Tinker Toy!"
Shouted Keesha and Jake.

"Next to me!" cried Nathan.
"Here, kitty," called Blake.

Then Mikaela scooted over
Right by Teacher's chair,
And she let Tinker share
Her carpet square.

"Kitty cats can't read,"
Explained Antoinette.
"They don't know their colors
Or the alphabet."

"They can't add two
Plus two!" yelled Cale.
"They're better at sleeping
Or chasing their tail."

Teacher said, "I think
Anyone can learn.
Let's give Tinker Toy
Her kindergarten turn.

"Her favorite foods
Are a mouse and a bird.
Can you name this critter?"

"ME-ow,"
  Tinker purred.

"Five little rabbits
Sleeping on a bed.
One fell off...."
"Me-OW!"
Tinker said.

"Foot fits in a shoe,
Hat sits on a head.
What else goes together?"
"ME-YOU," Tinker said.

Well, the kindergarten kids
Saw right from the start
That their Kindergarten Cat
Was kindergarten smart.

"Why, little Tinker Toy,"
Teacher said, "she's a whiz!
She's a *Thinker* Tinker Toy
Kind of cat, she is.

"Once she lived outside;
Now she'll stay indoors.
Look! She's making a bed
In our paintbrush drawers."

Then Teacher put on
Her Going-Home Coat
And she wrote on the board
This Going-Home note. . . .

"Let's sound it out
From beginning to end...."

Good-bye, Tinker Toy, our new kindergarten friend!

Tinker mewed good-bye.
What a long school day!
She thought, *I should put*
My crayons away.

Then she stretched times two,

And she yawned times three,

And she fell fast asleep
On the capital C.

And she dreamed of milk
In a golden bowl,
And she dreamed of mice
In a paw-sized hole,

And she dreamed of cats
Who like to roam,
But the very best dream
Was of kindergarten—
Home.